D0403950

# Morphine

•

## MIKHAIL BULGAKOV

A NEW DIRECTIONS PEARL

Manufactured in the United States of America
New Directions Books are printed on acid-free paper.
First published as a Pearl (NDP1266) by New Directions in 2013
Published simultaneously in Canada by Penguin Books Canada Limited
Design by Erik Rieselbach
Set in Albertina

Library of Congress Cataloging-in-Publication Data
Bulgakov, Mikhail, 1891–1940, author.
[Morfii. English]
Morphine / Mikhail Bulgakov ; translated by Hugh Aplin.
pages cm
"A New Directions Pearl."
ISBN 978-0-8112-2168-9 (alk. paper)
1. Morphine abuse—Fiction. 2. Drug addiction—Fiction.
I. Aplin, Hugh, translator. II. Title.
 PG3476.B78M6713 2013
 891.73'42—dc23
                    2013022867

10  9  8  7  6  5  4  3  2  1

New Directions Books are published for James Laughlin
by New Directions Publishing Corporation
80 Eighth Avenue, New York 10011

# MORPHINE

*I*

Clever people have been pointing out for a long time that happiness is like good health: when it's there, you don't notice it. But when the years have passed, how you do remember happiness, oh, how you do remember it!

As far as I'm concerned, I, as has now become apparent, was happy in 1917, in the winter. An unforgettable, headlong year of blizzards!

The incipient blizzard caught me up like a scrap of torn newspaper and carried me from my remote district to a small provincial town. What's so special, you might think, about a small provincial town? But if someone has sat, like me, in snow in the winter, and in stern, sorry woods in the summer, for a year and a half, without being away for a single day, if someone has ripped open the postal wrapping on the previous week's newspaper with beating heart, the way a happy lover does a light-blue envelope, if someone has travelled eighteen versts to a woman in labour in a sledge with horses harnessed in single file, he, one must assume, will understand me.*

*A verst was approximately equivalent to one kilometre. —Trans.

A kerosene lamp is a very cosy thing, but I'm in favour of electricity!

And now I saw them again, at last, seductive electric lamps! The little town's main street, well smoothed down by peasants' sledges, the street in which, enchanting one's gaze, there hung a shop sign with boots on it, a golden pretzel, red flags and an image of a young man with insolent little piggy eyes and an utterly unnatural hairstyle, signifying that housed behind the glass doors was the local Basile, who for thirty kopeks would undertake to shave you at anytime, with the exception of the public holidays in which my fatherland abounds.

To this day I recall with a tremor the Basile's napkins, napkins which persistently made me imagine the page in a German textbook on skin diseases, on which was depicted, with convincing clarity, a hard chancre on some citizen's chin.

But all the same, even those napkins cannot cloud my memories!

At the crossroads stood a live policeman; dimly visible in a dusty shop window were iron trays, bearing crowded rows of fancy cakes with ginger-coloured buttercream; hay covered the square; people walked, and rode, and conversed; on sale in a booth were the previous day's Moscow papers containing stunning news; nearby, the Moscow trains exchanged whistles of invitation. In a word, this was civilization, Babylon, Nevsky Avenue.

And that's to say nothing of the hospital. It had a surgical department, therapeutic, infectious diseases, obstetric departments. There was an operating room at the hospital, and in it was a gleaming autoclave, there was the silver of taps, the tables revealed their intricate damps; cogs, screws. There was a senior doctor at the hospital, three house surgeons (apart from me), *feldshers*, midwives, nurses, a pharmacy and a laboratory.* A laboratory, just think of it! With a Zeiss microscope and a fine supply of dyes.

I would shudder and turn cold, I was crushed by my impressions. Not a few days passed before I got used to the fact that the single-storey buildings of the hospital would blaze out in the December dusk, as if by command, with electric light.

It dazzled me. Water raged and thundered in the baths, and begrimed wooden thermometers dived and floated about in them. All day in the children's-infectious-diseases department there were groans bursting out, there was thin, pitiful crying and hoarse gurgling to be heard …

Nurses ran about, hurried around …

A heavy burden slipped from my soul. No longer did I bear a fateful responsibility for anything that might happen in the world. I wasn't to blame for a strangulated hernia, and I didn't shudder when a sledge arrived bringing a woman with a transverse lie, I wasn't concerned with cases of purulent pleurisy requiring operations … For the first time I felt like a human being, whose degree of

---

*A *feldsher* (from the German Feldscher, an army surgeon) was originally in the eighteenth century an assistant to a military surgeon in the field, but by the twentieth century had become an essential element in Russia's medical system, especially in rural areas, as a trained assistant to a doctor. —Trans.

responsibility was limited by some sort of framework. Childbirth? If you please, over there there's a rather low building, and over there is the last window, curtained with white gauze. The obstetrician is there, likeable and fat, with a little ginger moustache and rather bald. That's his business. Sledge, turn towards the window with the gauze! A compound fracture—that's the chief surgeon. Pneumonia? To Pavel Vladimirovich in the therapeutic department.

Oh, the majestic machine of a large hospital in regulated, precisely oiled motion! Like a new screw made to measure in advance, I too entered into the machinery and took on the children's department. Both diphtheria and scarlatina absorbed me and took up my days. But only the days. I began sleeping at night, because no longer was the ominous nocturnal knocking to be heard beneath my windows, the knocking which might get me up and carry me away into the darkness to danger and the inexorable.

In the evenings I started reading (about diphtheria and scarlatina in the first place, of course, and then, for some reason with strange interest, Fenimore Cooper) and was fully appreciative of the lamp over the desk, and of the grey coals on the tray with the samovar, and of the tea that grew cold, and of sleep after a sleepless year and a half . . .

Thus I was happy in the winter of 1917, having been transferred from a remote district of blizzards to a small provincial town.

## II

A month flew by, and after it a second and a third, 1917 receded, and February 1918 flew off. I had grown accustomed to my new position, and little by little began to forget my distant district. The green lamp with the hissing kerosene, the loneliness, the snowdrifts faded from my memory ... Ingrate! I forgot my battle post where, alone, without any support, I had struggled with illnesses unaided, getting out of the most bizarre situations like a Fenimore Cooper hero.

Occasionally, it's true, when I was going to bed with the pleasant thought of how in a moment I would fall asleep, certain scraps would fly by in my already darkening consciousness. A little green light, a twinkling lamp ... the squeaking of a sledge ... a short groan, then darkness, the muffled howling of the snowstorm in the fields ... Then it would all tumble aside and vanish ...

"I wonder who's sitting there now in my place? ... There must be someone ... A young doctor like me ... well, I sat my time out. February, March, April ... well, and let's say May—and that's the end of my probation period. And so at the end of May I shall part with my brilliant town and return to Moscow. And if the Revolution catches me up on its wing—I may have to travel some more … but in any event I shall never in my life see my rural district again … Never … The capital … A clinic … Asphalt, lights …"

That's what I thought.

"But all the same, it's a good thing that I spent the time in that district … I became a courageous person … I'm not afraid … What didn't I treat?! Yes, really? Eh? … I didn't treat any mental illness … I mean … actually no, I'm sorry … The agronomist drank himself to the devil that time … And I treated him, rather unsuccessfully too … Delirium tremens … How does that differ from a mental illness? I ought to read some psychiatry … Oh, to hell with it … Sometime later on, in Moscow … But now, first and foremost, it's paediatrics … and more paediatrics … and in particular the drudgery that is prescription-writing for children … Ugh, damn it … If a child's ten, then how much, let's say, pyramidon can it be given at a time? 0.1 or 0.15? … I've forgotten. And if the child's three? … Just paediatrics … and nothing more … enough of those mind-boggling surprises! Farewell, my rural district! … But why is the district coming to mind so insistently this evening? … The green light … I've settled my accounts with it for the rest of my life, haven't I … Enough now … Sleep …"

"There's a letter. It was brought by someone passing."

"Give it here."

The nurse was standing in my entrance hall. An overcoat with a threadbare collar had been thrown on over her white coat with its stamp on it. Snow was melting on the cheap blue envelope.

"Are you on duty in admissions today?" I asked with a yawn.

"I am."

"Is there no one there?"

"No, it's empty."

"Yif…"—a fit of yawning was tearing my mouth apart and making me pronounce words in a slovenly way—"anyone's brough' in … you jush let me know … I'm going to bed …"

"Very well. Can I go?"

"Yes, yes. You go."

She left. The door squealed, and I shuffled off in my slippers to the bedroom, my fingers tearing the envelope in a hideous, crooked way as I went.

Inside it was a crumpled, oblong prescription form bearing the blue stamp of my district, my hospital … An unforgettable form …

I grinned.

"That's interesting … I was thinking about the district all evening, and now it's turned up of its own accord to remind me of itself … A presentiment …"

Inscribed beneath the stamp in indelible pencil was a prescription. Latin words, illegible, crossed out …

"I don't understand a thing … A muddled prescription …"

I muttered, and stared at the word "*morphini* …" "Now what's the extraordinary thing about this prescription here? … Ah, yes … A four-per cent solution! Who on earth prescribes a four-per cent solution of morphine? … What for?!"

I turned the sheet of paper over and my yawning fit passed. Written in ink on the reverse of the sheet in a limp and well-spaced hand, was:

*11th February 1918.*

*Dear* collega!

*Forgive me for writing on this scrap. There's no paper to hand. I've fallen very gravely and badly ill. There's no one to help me, and I don't actually want to seek help from anyone but you.*

*For more than a month I've been working in your former district; I know you're in town and comparatively near me. In the name of our friendship and university years, I'm asking you to come to me quickly. If only for a day. If only for an hour. And if you tell me mine is a hopeless case, I'll believe you … But perhaps I can be saved? … Yes, perhaps I can still be saved? … Will there be a ray of hope for me? Please, don't inform anyone of the content of this letter.*

"Maria! Go to admissions straight away and send the duty nurse to me … What's her name? … Oh, I've forgotten … In short, the woman on duty who just brought me a letter. Quickly!"

"At once."

A few minutes later the nurse was standing in front of me, and snow was melting on the threadbare cat that served as the material for her collar.

"Who brought the letter?"

"I don't know. He had a beard. He's from the cooperative. He was going to town, he said."

"Hm ... well, off you go. No, hang on. I'll just write a note to the head doctor; please take it, and bring me back the reply."

"Very well."

My note to the head doctor:

*13th February 1918.*

*Respected Pavel Illarionovich. I've just received a letter from my university comrade Dr Polyakov. He's working in complete solitude at Gorelovo, my former district. He's fallen ill, evidently seriously. I consider it my duty to go to him. If you'll permit me, tomorrow I'll hand the department over for one day to Dr Rodovich and go and see Polyakov. The man is helpless.*
*Respectfully yours,*

*Dr Bomgard.*

The head doctor's note in reply:

*Respected Vladimir Mikhailovich, do go.*

*Petrov.*

I spent the evening studying a guide to the railways. Gorelovo could be reached thus: by leaving next day at two o'clock in the afternoon on the Moscow post train, travelling thirty versts on the railway, getting off at the station of N***, and from there going twenty-two versts by sledge to the Gorelovo Hospital.

"With luck I'll be at Gorelovo tomorrow night," I thought, lying in bed. "What's he got? Typhus, pneumonia? Neither of them ... Had that been the case he would have written simply: "I've got pneumonia." But here you have a confused, somewhat insincere letter ... "Gravely ... and badly ill ..." What with? Syphilis? Yes, it's syphilis, without a doubt. He's horrified ... he's concealing it ... he's afraid ... But what horses, I'd like to know, am I to use to travel to Gorelovo from the station? That'll be good, when I arrive at the station in the dusk, and there's no transport for me to use to reach him ... But no. I'll find a way. I'll find someone with horses at the station. Or send a telegram for him to send out horses! No point! The telegram will arrive a day after I get there ... It won't fly through the air to Gorelovo, after all. It'll be lying at the station until there's someone to take it. I know that Gorelovo. Oh, it's a godforsaken spot!"

The letter on the form lay on my night table in the circle of light from the lamp, and next to it was the companion of my irritable insomnia with its stubble of cigarette butts, the ashtray. I tossed and turned on my crumpled sheet, and vexation sprang up in my soul. The letter began to irritate me.

"After all, if it's nothing acute, but, let's say, syphilis, then why ever doesn't he come here himself? Why should I race through a blizzard to him? What, will I cure him of lues in one evening, or something? Or of cancer of the oesophagus? What am I talking about, cancer! He's two years younger than me. He's twenty-five ... "Gravely ..." A sarcoma? It's a ridiculous, hysterical letter. A letter that might give the recipient a migraine ... And there it is. Tightening the vein on my temple ... So you'll wake in the morning, and it'll go up from the vein to your crown, it'll fetter half your head, and by evening you'll be swallowing pyramidon and caffeine. And what are you going to be like in the sledge with pyramidon?! You'll have to get a travelling fur coat from the *feldsher*, you'll freeze in your overcoat tomorrow ... What's the matter with him? "Will there be a ray of hope ..."—people write like that in novels, but certainly not in serious doctors' letters! ... Sleep, sleep ... Don't think about it any more. Everything will become clear tomorrow ... Tomorrow."

I turned the switch off, and the darkness devoured my room instantly. Sleep ... The vein is aching ... But I have no right to get angry with a man over a ridiculous letter when I don't yet know what's wrong. A man is suffering in his own particular way, and here he is writing to another. Well, in the way he knows, the way he understands ...

And it's unworthy to denigrate him, even in my mind, because of a migraine, because of anxiety. Maybe it's neither an insincere, nor a novelish letter. I haven't seen him for two years, Seryozha Polyakov, but I remember him very well. He was always a very sensible man ... Yes. That means some kind of misfortune has befallen him ... And my vein feels better ... Sleep's evidently on its way. What's the mechanism of sleep? ... I read about it in a book on physiology ... but it's an obscure business ... I don't understand what sleep means ... how do the brain cells fall asleep?! I'll tell you in confidence, I don't understand it. And for some reason I'm sure that even the compiler of that book on physiology himself isn't very definitely sure either ... One theory's as good as another ... There's Seryozha Polyakov standing over a zinc table in a green double-breasted jacket with gold buttons, and on the table is a corpse ...

Hm, yes ... now that's a dream ...

# III

Knock, knock … Bang, bang, bang … Aba … Who is it? Who is it? What is it? … Oh, someone's knocking, oh, damn, someone's knocking … Where am I? What am I doing? … What's the matter? Yes, in my own bed … Why on earth are they waking me up? They have every right, because I'm on duty. Wake up, Dr Bomgard. There goes Maria, shuffling to the door to open up. What's the time? Half-past twelve … It's night-time. So I was asleep for only an hour. How's the migraine? It's there. There it is!

There was a quiet knock at the door.

"What's the matter?"

I opened the door into the dining room just a little. The nurse's face looked at me from the darkness, and I made out at once that it was pale, that the eyes were widened, agitated.

"Who's been brought in?"

"The doctor from the Gorelovo district," the nurse replied in a loud, hoarse voice. "The doctor's shot himself."

"Pol-ya-kov? That's not possible! Polyakov?!"

"I don't know his name."

"Listen … I'm on my way now, right now. And you run to the head doctor, wake him up this second. Tell him I'm summoning him urgently to admissions."

The nurse rushed off—and the white blot vanished from my eyes.

Two minutes later the angry blizzard, dry and prickly, lashed my cheeks on the porch, blew out the skirts of my overcoat and turned my frightened body to ice.

In the windows of the admissions ward blazed a white, restless light. On the porch, in a cloud of snow, I ran into the senior doctor who was speeding to the same place as me.

"Your man? Polyakov?" asked the surgeon, coughing a little.

"I can't understand a thing. It's evidently him," I replied, and we speedily went into admissions.

A woman, all wrapped up, rose from a bench to meet us. Familiar, tearstained eyes looked at me from under the bottom of a brown headscarf. I recognized Maria Vlasyevna, a midwife from Gorelovo, my faithful assistant during childbirth at the Gorelovo Hospital.

"Polyakov?" I asked.

"Yes," replied Maria Vlasyevna, "it was awful, Doctor, I was trembling all the way as I was driving, I just had to get him here …"

"When?"

"This morning at dawn," muttered Maria Vlasyevna, "a watchman came running and says … 'There's been a shot in the doctor's apartment …'"

Under a lamp, which shed a horrid, alarming light, lay Dr. Polyakov, and from my very first glance at the soles of his felt boots, lifeless, as though made of stone, my heart missed a beat in its customary way.

His hat was removed, revealing damp hair, all stuck together. Hands began flashing over Polyakov, my hands, the nurse's and Maria Vlasyevna's, and white gauze with spreading yellow and red patches emerged from under his overcoat. His chest was rising weakly. I felt his pulse and faltered, the pulse kept disappearing under my fingers, stretching out and breaking into a thread with little knots, frequent and fragile. The surgeon's hand was already stretching out towards his shoulder, pinching the pale body at the shoulder in order to inject camphor. And here the wounded man parted his lips, at which a pinkish bloody stripe appeared on them, and stirring his blue lips a little, in a dry, weak voice he said:

"Don't bother with camphor. To hell with it."

"Be quiet," the surgeon answered him and squeezed the yellow oil in under the skin.

"One has to assume that the pericardial sac's been affected," whispered Maria Vlasyevna, taking a firm grip on the edge of the table and starting to peer at the wounded man's unending eyelids (his eyes were closed). Violet-grey shadows, like the shadows of sunset, began to blossom ever more vividly in the depressions by the wings of his nose, and little beads of sweat, as if of mercury, were standing out like dew on the shadows.

"A revolver?" asked the surgeon, with a twitch of his cheek.

"A Browning," babbled Maria Vlasyevna.

"O-oh dear," the surgeon said all of a sudden, crossly, so it seemed, and in vexation, then flapped his hand and moved away.

I turned to him in fright, not understanding. There was the flash of someone else's eyes over my shoulder. Another doctor had come too.

Polyakov suddenly shifted his mouth crookedly, like someone feeling sleepy who wants to get rid of a persistent fly, and then his lower jaw started moving as though he were choking on a little lump of something and wanted to swallow it. Ah, anyone who has seen bad revolver or rifle wounds is very familiar with that movement! Maria Vlasyevna frowned painfully and sighed.

"Dr Bomgard," said Polyakov, barely audibly.

"I'm here," I whispered, and the sound of my voice was gentle, right beside his lips.

"The notebook's for you …" Polyakov responded, his voice hoarse and weaker still.

At that point he opened his eyes and raised them to the room's joyless ceiling, receding into darkness. His dark pupils began filling with light as though from within, and the whites of his eyes seemed to become transparent, bluish. His eyes came to a halt on high, then grew dull and lost that fleeting beauty.

Dr Polyakov was dead.

It's night. Close to dawn. The lamp burns very clearly, because the little town is sleeping and there's a lot of electric current. All is silent, and Polyakov's body is in the chapel. It's night.

On the desk in front of my eyes, which are sore from reading, lie an opened envelope and a sheet of paper.

On the latter is written:

*Dear comrade!*
*I'm not going to wait for you. I've changed my mind about having treatment. It's hopeless. And I don't want to suffer any more either. I've had enough. I caution others: be careful with white crystals dissolved in twenty-five parts of water. I put too much trust in them and they have been my undoing. I'm giving you my diary. You always seemed to me an inquisitive man and a lover of human documents. If you're interested, read my medical record.*
*Farewell. Yours,*
        *S. Polyakov.*

A postscript in large letters:

*Please don't blame anyone for my death.*
*Physician Sergei Polyakov.*
              *13th February 1918.*

Next to the suicide's letter is a notebook in black oilcloth, a sort of commonplace book. The first half of its pages has been torn out of it. In the remaining half there are short entries, at first in pencil or ink and in a small, precise hand, and at the end of the book in indelible pencil and a thick, red one and in a careless hand, a jumpy hand, and with a lot of abbreviated words.

## IV

*… 7\*, 20th January.*

… and I'm very glad. And thank God, the more remote, the better. I can't bear to see anyone, and here I *shan't* see anyone, other than sick peasants. But they won't trouble my wound in any way, will they? Others, incidentally, have been planted out in zemstvo districts much like me.† My entire cohort of graduates, those not liable for call-up to the War (second category conscripts from 1916), have been distributed among the zemstvos. But that's of no interest to anyone. Of my friends, I've learnt only of Ivanov and Bomgard. Ivanov chose Archangel Province (a matter of taste), while Bomgard, as the female *feldsher* told me, is working in a remote district like mine, three districts away from me in Gorelovo. I was meaning to write to him, but changed my mind. I don't want to see or hear from anyone.

*\*Undoubtedly 1917. —Dr. Bomgard*

†A zemstvo was a district or provincial assembly with certain local administrative powers. —Trans.

*21st January.*

A blizzard. Nothing.

*25th January.*

What a clear sunset. Migrainin—a combination of *antipirin, coffein* and *ac. citric.*

1.0 per powder ... is 1.0 permissible? It is.

*3rd February.*

I received last week's newspapers today. I didn't start reading them, but was drawn, all the same, to have a look at the theatres section. *Aida* was on last week. That means she emerged onto a dais and sang: "Come, dearest friend, draw near to me ..."*

She has an extraordinary voice, and how strange it is that a clear, huge voice has been given to a dark little soul ...

[Here there is a break, two or three pages have been torn out.]

...of course it's unworthy, Dr Polyakov. And it's schoolboy stupidity to use the language of the marketplace to attack a woman because she's gone! She doesn't want to stay—she's gone. And that's an end to it. How simple it all is, in essence. An opera singer took up with a young doctor, stayed with him for a year, and now she's gone.

---

*A line sung by Amneris, the Pharoah's daughter, to Aida, the captured Ethiopian princess who is Amneris's rival for the affections of the soldier Radames, in act 1 of Verdi's opera *Aida.* —Trans.

Kill her? Kill? Oh, how stupid, empty it all is. It's hopeless! I don't want to think. Don't want to …

*11th February.*

Blizzards and more blizzards … I'm being snowed in! For evenings on end I'm alone, alone. I light the lamp and sit there. In the daytime I do still see people. But I work mechanically. I've grown accustomed to the work. It's not as terrifying as I used to think. Actually, the military hospital in the War helped me a lot. I came here not entirely illiterate after all.

Today I performed the operation of version for the first time.

And so, there are three people buried here beneath the snow: me, Anna Kirillovna, who's a *feldsher* and midwife, and a male *feldsher*. He's married. They (the assistant staff) live in the wing. But I'm alone.

*15th February.*

Last night an interesting thing happened. I was getting ready for bed, when suddenly I had pains in the region of the stomach. But what pains! My forehead came out in a cold sweat. Our medicine is, after all, a dubious science, I have to say. What can make a man who has absolutely no ailment of the stomach or intestines (e.g. append.), who has a splendid liver and kidneys, whose intestines are functioning perfectly normally, have such pains in the night that he starts rolling around on his bed?

Groaning, I got as far as the kitchen, where the cook

and her husband, Vlas, spend the nights. I sent Vlas to Anna Kirillovna. She came to me in the night and was forced to give me a morphine injection. She says I was absolutely green. Why?

I don't like our *feldsher*. He's unsociable, whereas Anna Kirillovna is a very nice and mature person. I'm amazed at how a woman of no age can live in complete solitude in this snowy coffin. Her husband is a prisoner of the Germans.

I cannot but give praise to the first man to extract morphine from poppy heads. A true benefactor of mankind. The pains ceased seven minutes after the injection. It's interesting: the pains were coming in one complete wave, without allowing any pauses, so that I was positively gasping for breath, as if someone were twisting a scorching crowbar that had been driven into my belly. Four minutes or so after the injection I began to discern an undulatory nature to the pain:

It would be a very good thing if a doctor had the opportunity of testing many a medicine on himself. He would have a completely different understanding of their effect. After the injection, for the first time in recent months I had a good, deep sleep—without any thoughts of the woman who deceived me.

*16th February.*

At surgery today Anna Kirillovna enquired how I felt, and said this was the first occasion in all this time that she'd seen me cheerful.

"Am I cheerless, then?"

"Very," she replied with conviction, and added that she was astounded by the fact that I was always silent.

"That's just the sort of man I am."

But that's a lie. I was a man full of *joie de vivre* until my domestic drama.

The dusk gathers early. I'm alone in the apartment. Pain came in the evening, but not great pain, like a shadow of yesterday's, somewhere behind my breastbone. Fearing the return of yesterday's attack, I injected one centigram into my thigh myself.

The pain ceased almost instantly. It's a good thing Anna Kirillovna left the phial.

*18th.*

Four injections are nothing to worry about.

*25th February.*

That Anna Kirillovna's an odd one! As though I'm not a doctor, 1 ½ syringes = 0.015 *morph.*? Yes.

*1st March*.

Dr Polyakov, be careful!

Nonsense.

*Dusk*.

But for already a couple of weeks now, my thoughts haven't once returned to the woman who deceived me. The motif from her role, Amneris, has left me. I'm very proud of this. I'm a man.

Anna K. has become my secret wife. It couldn't possibly have been otherwise. We're imprisoned on an uninhabited island.

The snow has changed, it seems to have become greyer. There are no more really hard frosts, but the blizzards do resume at times …

The first minute: a sensation of something touching my neck. This touch becomes warm and expands. In the second minute a cold wave suddenly passes through the pit of my stomach, and following that there begins an extraordinary clarification of my thought and an explosion of my capacity for work. Absolutely all unpleasant sensations cease. This is the high point of the manifestation of man's spiritual power. And if I hadn't been ruined by a medical education, I would have said that a man can only work properly after an injection of morphine. Truly: what damned use is a man if the slightest little neuralgia can completely knock him out of the saddle!

Anna K. is scared. I reassured her, saying that ever since I was a child I've been noted for the most enormous strength of will.

*2nd March.*

Rumours of something stupendous. Nicholas II has allegedly been toppled.

I go to bed very early. At about nine o'clock. And sleep sweetly.

*10th March.*

There's a revolution going on there. The day has become longer, but the dusk seems to be a little bluer.

Never before have I had such dreams at dawn. They're double dreams.

What's more, the principal one, I'd say, is made of glass. It's transparent.

And so, then—I dream of an eerily lit lamp, and out of it blazes a multicoloured ribbon of lights. Amneris is waving a green feather and singing. The orchestra, utterly unearthly, is extraordinarily sonorous. I can't convey it in words, though. In short, in a normal dream music is soundless … (in a normal one? That's another question, which dream is more normal?! I'm joking, though …)

soundless, but in my dream it's quite sublimely audible. And the main thing is that, using my will, I can amplify or soften the music. I seem to recall in *War and Peace* there's a description of how Petya Rosrov, when half asleep, experienced the same state.* Leo Tolstoy's a remarkable writer!

Now about the transparency: so, then, showing completely realistically through the play of colours of Aida are the edge of my desk, which I can see from the door of the study, the lamp and the glossy floor, and bursting through the wave of the Bolshoi Theatre's orchestra I can hear clear footsteps, treading pleasantly like muffled castanets.

So it's eight o'clock, and this is Anna K. coming to my room to wake me up and tell me what's going on in the surgery.

She doesn't realize that I don't need waking, that I can hear everything and can talk to her.

And yesterday I did this experiment:

*Anna*—Sergei Vasilyevich …

*I*—I can hear … (*quietly to the music: "louder"*).

The music. —a grand chord. D sharp …

*Anna*—Twenty people have registered.

*Amneris*—(*sings*).

It can't be conveyed on paper though.

Are these dreams harmful? Oh no. After them I get up strong and in good spirits. And I work well. I'm even taking an interest now, whereas I wasn't before. And no won-

*Volume 4, part 3, chapter 10. —Trans.

der, all my thoughts were concentrated on my ex-wife.

But now I'm calm.

I'm calm.

*19th March.*

In the night I had a quarrel with Anna K.

"I'm not going to prepare the solution any more."

I started to try and persuade her.

"Nonsense, Annusya. What, a little boy, am I?"

"I'm not going to. You'll die."

"Well, as you wish. But you must understand that I've got pains in my chest!"

"Have treatment."

"Where?"

"Go away on leave. Morphine isn't treatment." (Then she had a think and added …) "I can't forgive myself for preparing the second bottle for you that time."

"What, I'm a morphine addict, am I?"

"Yes, you're becoming one."

"So you're not going to go?"

"No."

Here, for the first time, I discovered in myself an unpleasant capacity to get angry and, most importantly, shout at people when I'm in the wrong.

However, it wasn't at once. I went into the bedroom. Had a look. There was barely a splash at the bottom of the bottle. I drew it into a syringe—it proved to be a quarter full. I hurled the syringe down, almost breaking it, and started to tremble. Picked it up carefully and examined it—not a single crack. I sat in the bedroom for about twenty minutes. When I went out again, she wasn't there.

She'd gone.

Imagine—I couldn't bear it, I went to see her. I knocked at the lighted window in her wing. She came out onto the porch wrapped up in a scarf. The night was ever so quiet. The snow fluffy. Somewhere far away in the sky there was a breath of spring.

"Anna Kirillovna, be so good as to give me the keys to the pharmacy."

She whispered:

"No, I won't."

"Comrade, be so good as to give me the keys to the pharmacy. I'm speaking to you as a doctor."

I could see in the dusk that her face altered, she turned very white, while her eyes deepened, sank, turned black. And she replied in a voice that made pity stir in my soul.

But straight away anger surged over me again.

She:

"Why do you talk like that, why? Ah, Sergei Vasilycvich, I'm acting out of pity for you."

And at this point she freed her hands from under the scarf, and I could see that she had the keys in her hands. So she had come out to me and brought them with her.

I (rudely):

"Give me the keys!"

I tore them out of her hands.

And I set off over the rotten, bouncing planked footway towards the white building of the hospital.

Fury was sizzling in my soul, first and foremost because I have absolutely no idea at all of how to prepare a morphine solution for subcutaneous injection. I'm a doctor, not a *feldsher*!

I shook as I walked.

And I could hear that, behind me, like a faithful dog, she had set off too. And tenderness shot up inside me, but I suppressed it. I turned and, baring my teeth, said:

"Are you going to do it or not?"

And she flapped a hand like someone doomed, as if to say "it's all the same," and answered quietly:

"Let me do it …"

… An hour later I was in a reasonable state. Of course, I begged her pardon for my senseless rudeness. I didn't know myself what had come over me. I used to be a polite person before.

Her response to my apology was strange. She went down on her knees, pressed herself up against my hands and said:

"I'm not cross with you. No. I already know now that you're done for. I know it. And I curse myself for having given you the injection that time."

I calmed her as best I could, assuring her that she had absolutely nothing to do with this and that I myself was answerable for my actions. I promised her that from to-morrow I would seriously begin breaking the habit by de-creasing the dose.

"How much have you just injected?"

"A silly amount: Three syringes of one-per cent solution."

She took her head in her hands and fell silent.

"Don't you worry!"

… In essence, I can understand her anxiety. *Morphinum hydrochloricum* is, indeed, a formidable thing. The habit for it forms very quickly. But a little habit isn't morphine ad-diction, is it? …

… To tell the truth, that woman is the only person who is genuinely faithful to me. And in essence, she really ought to be my wife. I've forgotten the other one. Forgotten her. And for that, after all, it's thank you to the morphine …

*8th April 1917.*

It's agony.

*9th April.*

The spring is dreadful.

The Devil in a bottle. Cocaine is the Devil in a bottle.

This is its effect:

Almost instantly after injecting one syringeful of two-per cent solution, a state of calm sets in which turns straight away into delight and bliss. But this continues for only one or two minutes. And then it's all lost without trace, as if it had never been. Pain, dread, darkness set in. The spring roars, black birds fly from bare branch to bare branch, while in the distance the forest reaches towards the sky like bristles, broken and black, and beyond it, encompassing a quarter of the sky, there burns the first sunset of spring.

I pace the big, lonely, empty room in the doctor's apartment diagonally, from the doors to the window and from the window to the doors. How many such walks can I take? Fifteen or sixteen—no more. And then I have to turn and go into the bedroom. The syringe is lying on some gauze next to the bottle. I pick it up and, carelessly rubbing some iodine onto my thigh, which is covered in needle marks, I plunge the needle into my skin. There's no pain. Oh, on the contrary: I'm anticipating the euphoria that will soon be coming. And then it does come. I know of it because the sounds of the accordion which Vlas the watchman, rejoicing at spring, is playing on the porch, the ragged, hoarse sounds of the accordion, which come flying to me, muffled, through the window pane, become angelic voices, and the rough basses in billowing furs hum like a heavenly choir. But then, after an instant, obeying some mysterious law which isn't described in a single one of the pharmacology books, the cocaine in the blood is transformed into something new. I know: it's a mixture of the Devil and my blood. And on the porch Vlas flags, and I hate him, while the sunset, with an uneasy rumbling, scorches my innards. And that's how it is several times running in the course of an evening until I realize that I'm poisoned. My heart starts thumping such that I can feel it in my arms, in my temples … and then it sinks into an abyss, and there are sometimes moments when I think that Dr Polyakov won't come back to life again …

*13th April.*

I—the unfortunate Dr Polyakov, who in February of this year fell ill with morphine addiction—warn all those to whose lot a fate such as mine falls not to try substituting cocaine for morphine. Cocaine is the most horrible and insidious poison. Yesterday Anna barely nursed me back with camphor, and today I'm a semi-corpse …

*6th May 1917.*

I haven't touched my diary in quite a long time. And that's a pity. In essence, it isn't a diary but a medical record, and I evidently feel professionally drawn to my only friend in the world (if you don't count my mournful and often tearful friend Anna).

And so, if I'm to write a medical record, then here: I'm injecting myself with morphine twice a day, at five o'clock in the afternoon (after dinner) and at twelve midnight, before going to bed.

A three-per cent solution: two syringefuls. Consequently, I'm getting 0.06 at a time.

Quite a bit!

My earlier notes were somewhat hysterical. There's nothing in particular to worry about. It doesn't affect my capacity for work at all. On the contrary, I live all day on the nocturnal injection of the day before. I manage operations magnificently, I'm irreproachably attentive to the principles of prescription-writing, and give my word as a doctor that my morphine addiction has done my patients no harm. But there's something else that's tormenting me. It constantly seems to me that somebody will find out about my vice. And I find it difficult during surgery, feeling the hard, searching gaze of my assistant *feldsher* on my back.

Nonsense! He hasn't guessed. Nothing gives me away. It's only in the evening that my pupils might betray me, but I never encounter him in the evening.

I've replenished the quite awful depletion of morphine in our pharmacy after a trip to the local town. But even there I had to endure some unpleasant moments. The manager of the store took my order, in which I had also prudently included all sorts of other nonsense like caffeine (of which we have as much as you like), and said:

"Forty grams of morphine?"

And I sense that I'm averting my eyes like a schoolboy. I sense that I'm blushing …

He says:

"We don't have such a quantity. I'll give you ten grams or so."

And he *doesn't* have it, it's true, but it seems to me that he has penetrated my secret, that his eyes are probing and drilling into me, and I am agitated and suffering.

No, it's the pupils, only the pupils that are dangerous, and for that reason I shall make it a rule not to encounter people in the evening, in that respect, incidentally, a more convenient place than my district couldn't be found; I haven't seen anyone but my patients for more than six months now.

And I'm absolutely nothing to them.

*18th May.*

It's a stuffy night. There's going to be a storm. The black belly in the distance beyond the forest is growing and swelling. And there it is, a pale and alarming flash. The storm's coming.

There's a book in front of my eyes, and it says in it, regarding abstinence from morphine:

> … great anxiety, a state of disquiet and depression, irritability, deterioration of the memory, sometimes hallucinations and, to a limited extent, blackouts …

I haven't experienced hallucinations, but regarding the remainder I can say: oh, what tame, banal words, words that say nothing! "A state of depression"! …

No, having fallen sick with this dreadful illness, I warn doctors to be more compassionate towards their patients. It's not "a state of depression," but a slow death that takes hold of a morphine addict, as soon as you deprive him of morphine for an hour or two. The air is insubstantial, it can't be swallowed ... there isn't a cell in the body that doesn't thirst ... For what? That can be neither defined nor explained. In short, the man is gone. He's switched off. It's a corpse that moves, yearns, suffers. He wants nothing, thinks about nothing but morphine. Morphine!

Death from thirst is a heavenly, blissful one in comparison with the thirst for morphine. This is probably the way someone buried alive tries to catch the last, insignificant little air bubbles in the coffin and tears the skin on his chest with his nails. This is the way a heretic at the stake groans and stirs when the first tongues of flame lick at his feet ...

Death—a dry, slow death ...

That's what lies beneath those professorial words "a state of depression".

I can't go on. And so I've just gone and injected myself. A deep breath. Another deep breath.

That's better. But now ... now ... there's the minty chill in the pit of my stomach ...

Three syringefuls of a three-per cent solution. That'll last me until midnight ...

Rubbish. That entry is rubbish. It's not so terrible. Sooner or later I'll give it up! ... But now I've got to sleep, sleep.

I'm simply tormenting and weakening myself with this silly struggle with morphine.

[Hereafter a couple of dozen pages have been cut out of the notebook.]

… *ber*

… ain vomiting at 4.30.

When I'm feeling better I'll note down my dreadful impressions.

*14th November 1917.*

And so, after fleeing from Dr …'s [the name has been thoroughly crossed out] clinic in Moscow, I'm at home again. The rain is pouring down in sheets and hiding the world from me. And let it hide it from me. I don't need it, just as no one in the world needs me. I lived through shooting and revolt while I was in the clinic. But the idea of giving up the treatment had furtively ripened inside me even before the fighting on the streets of Moscow. Thank you, morphine, for making me brave. I'm not afraid of any shooting. And what is there in general that can frighten a man who thinks of only one thing—of the wonderful, divine crystals. When the *feldsher*, completely terrorized by the booming of cannons …

[Here a page has been torn out.]

…rn out this page so that nobody would read the shameful description of the way a man with a degree fled furtively, like a coward, and stole his own suit.

The suit—that's nothing!

I took a hospital shirt. There were other things on my mind. The next day, after having an injection, I came back to life and returned to Dr N. He greeted me compassionately, but there was contempt showing through the compassion all the same. And that was wrong. After all, he's a psychiatrist, and he ought to understand that I'm not always in control of myself. I'm ill. Why should he feel contempt for me? I returned the hospital shirt.

He said:

"Thank you," and added: "What are you thinking of doing now?"

I said cheerily (at that moment I was in a state of euphoria):

"I've decided to go back to my place in the backwoods, particularly as my leave has run out. I'm very grateful to you for your help, I feel significantly better. I'll continue the treatment at home."

This was his reply:

"You don't feel a bit better. I really do find it funny that you can say that to me. I mean, just one look at your pupils is enough. Who do you think you're talking to? ..."

"I can't break the habit all at once, Professor ... now in particular, when all these events are taking place ... the shooting has completely unnerved me ..."

"It's over. There's a new regime. Come back into the clinic."

At that point I remembered everything ... the cold corridors ... the empty walls, painted with oil paints ... and I'm crawling like a dog with a broken leg ... waiting for something ... What? A hot bath? ... An injection of 0.005 of morphine. A dose of which no one dies, it's true ... but only … yet all the depression remains, it lies like a burden, just as it did before … The empty nights, the shirt I was wearing and ripped to pieces, begging to be let out? …

No. No. Morphine was invented, it was extracted from the dried, rattling heads of a divine plant, so find a way of treating people without tormenting them too! I shook my head stubbornly. At this point he started to rise, and I suddenly flung myself towards the door in fright. I thought he wanted to lock the door behind me and keep me in the clinic by force …

The Professor turned crimson.

"I'm not a prison governor," he said, not without irritation, "and this isn't Butyrki.* Sit quietly. You were boasting that you were completely normal two weeks ago. And yet …"—he expressively repeated my gesture of fright— "I'm not holding you here, sir."

"Professor, give me back the paper I signed. I beg of you," and my voice even had a pitiful quaver to it.

"Certainly."

He gave a click with a key in the desk and gave me back the document I had signed (about my pledging to follow the entire two-month course of treatment, and their being able to detain me at the clinic, etc., in short, of the usual kind).

I took the note with a trembling hand and put it away, murmuring:

*Moscow's most famous prison. —Trans.

"Thank you."

Then I stood up to leave. And started to go.

"Dr Polyakov!" rang out in my wake. I turned, holding on to the door handle. "Look here," he began, "think again. You must understand that you'll find yourself back in the psychiatric clinic all the same, albeit a little later on … And, what's more, you'll be in a much worse state. I've been dealing with you as with a doctor, after all. But when you come back then, you'll already be in a state of complete mental collapse. Essentially, my friend, you shouldn't be practising, and it's probably criminal not to notify your place of work."

I winced and felt distinctly that the colour had drained from my face (though I have very little of it to begin with).

"I beg you, Professor," I said in a muffled voice, "not to say anything to anyone … Why, I'll be dismissed … stigmatized as a sick man … Why would you want to do that to me?"

"Go," he cried in vexation, "go. I won't say anything. You'll be sent back all the same …"

I left, and I swear I was twitching in pain and shame for the entire journey … Why? …

It's very simple. Ah, my friend, my faithful diary. You won't give me away, will you? It isn't a matter of the suit, but of my stealing morphine at the clinic. Three-cubic centimetres in crystals and ten grams of one-per cent solution.

That's not the only thing that interests me, there's this

too. The key was sticking out of the cabinet. Well, and what if it hadn't been there? Would I have forced the cabinet open or not? Eh? If I'm honest?

Yes, I would.

And so, Dr Polyakov is a thief. There'll be ample time for me to tear the page out.

Well, as regards my practising though, he did go too far. Yes, I'm a degenerate. Absolutely true. The disintegration of my moral being has started. But I can work, I can't do any evil or harm to any of my patients.

Yes, why did I steal? It's very simple. I decided that during the fighting and all the commotion connected with the revolt, I wouldn't get hold of any morphine anywhere. But when it calmed down, I got hold of another fifteen grams of one-per cent solution in a chemist's on the outskirts of town—which for me is useless and tedious (I'll have to inject nine syringefuls!). And I had to demean myself too. The pharmacist demanded an official stamp, and the looks he gave me were sullen and suspicious. But on the other hand, the next day, when back to normal, I got twenty grams in crystals at another chemist's without any delay at all— wrote an order for the hospital (and at the same time, of course, ordered caffeine and aspirin). Yes, when all's said and done, why should I hide and be afraid? Indeed, as though I had it written on my forehead that I'm a morphine addict? Whose business is it, when all's said and done?

And is the disintegration so great? I adduce these diary entries as witnesses. They're fragmented, but after all, I'm not a writer! There aren't any crazy ideas in them, are there? I think my reasoning is perfectly sound.

A morphine addict has one piece of good fortune, which nobody can take away from him—the capacity to spend his life in total solitude. And solitude means important, significant ideas, it means contemplation, tranquillity, wisdom ...

The night flows by, black and silent. Somewhere out there is the forest, stripped bare, and beyond it are the river, cold, autumn.

Far, far away is dishevelled, turbulent Moscow. I don't care about anything, I don't need anything, and I'm not drawn to go anywhere.

Burn, light, inside my lamp, burn quietly, I want to rest after the adventures of Moscow, I want to forget them.

And I have.

I have.

*18th November.*

Light frosts. It's dried up. I went out for a walk down the path towards the river, because I hardly ever get a breath of air.

Even if my being is disintegrating, I'm making attempts, all the same, to abstain from it. This morning, for example,

I didn't do any injecting. (I'm now injecting three syringe-fuls of four-per cent solution three times a day.) It's awkward. I'm sorry for Anna. Every new per cent is killing her. I'm sorry. Oh, what a person!

Yes … right … so … when I began to feel bad, I decided nonetheless to torment myself a bit (if only Professor N. could see me) by delaying the injection, and I set off towards the river.

What a wilderness. Not a sound, not a rustle. There's no dusk yet, but it's there somewhere, hiding, and it's creeping over the marshes, over the hummocks, between the tree stumps … It's coming, coming to the Levkovo Hospital … And I'm creeping along, leaning on a stick (to tell the truth, I've grown somewhat weaker of late).

And then I see that, flying swiftly up the slope from the river towards me, without moving her legs beneath her many-coloured bell-shaped skirt, is a little old woman with yellow hair … For the first few moments I didn't understand who she was and wasn't even frightened. A little old woman like any other. Strange—why is the old woman bareheaded and wearing only a blouse in the cold? … And then: where's the old woman from? Who is she? When our surgery at Levkovo is over and the last peasants' sledges go their different ways, there's no one for ten versts all around. Mists, marshes, forests! And then suddenly cold sweat started running down my back—I understood! The little old woman wasn't running, but actually *flying*, not touching the ground. Nice? Yet that wasn't the thing that tore a cry from me, but the fact that in the old woman's hands there was a pitchfork.

Why was I so frightened? Why? I fell onto one knee, holding my hands out, shielding myself, so as not to see her, then I turned and, hobbling, ran towards home, as to a place of salvation, not wishing for anything other than for my heart not to burst, and for my soon to be running into warm rooms and seeing Anna alive … and for morphine …

And I ran back.


Nonsense. A trivial hallucination. A chance hallucination.


*19th November.*
   Vomiting. This is bad.


My nocturnal conversation with Anna on the 21st.
   *Anna*—The *feldsher* knows.
   *I*—Really? I don't care. It's nothing.
   *Anna*—If you don't leave here and go to town, I'll hang myself. Do you hear? Look at your hands, look at them.
   *I*—They're trembling a little. It doesn't prevent me from working at all.
   *Anna*—Will you look—they're transparent. Just bone and skin … Take a look at your face … Listen, Seryozha.
   Go away, I implore you, go away …
   *I*—What about you?
   *Anna*—Go away. Go away. You're dying.
   *I*—Well, that's overstating it. But I really can't understand myself why I've grown weak so quickly. After all, I haven't been ill for a full year yet. It's evidently my constitution.

*Anna (sadly)*—What can bring you back to life? Perhaps that Amneris of yours—your wife?

*I*—Oh no. You can relax. Thank you to the morphine, it rid me of her. Instead of her there's morphine.

*Anna*—Oh my God … what am I going to do?

I thought there were people like Anna only in novels. And if I ever recover, I shall throw in my lot with her for good. May the other not return from Germany.

*27th December.*

I haven't picked up my notebook in a long time. I'm all wrapped up, and the horses are waiting. Bomgard has gone from the Gorelovo district, and I've been sent to replace him. A woman doctor's coming to my district.

Anna's here … She'll come and visit me …

Even if it is thirty versts.

We've come to a firm decision that from 1st January I shall take a month's sick leave and go to the Professor in Moscow. I'll sign another document, and I'll suffer a month of inhuman torment at his clinic.

Farewell, Levkovo. Anna, goodbye.

*1918.*

January.

I didn't go. I can't part with my crystalline, soluble idol. I shall die during treatment.

And it occurs to me more and more often that I don't *need* treatment.

*15th January.*

Vomiting in the morning.

Three syringefuls of four-per cent solution at dusk.

Three syringefuls of four-per cent solution in the night.

*16th January.*

An operating day, and so great abstinence—from the night until six o'clock in the evening.

At dusk—the most dreadful time—when already in my apartment, I distinctly heard a voice, monotonous and menacing, repeating:

"Sergei Vasilyevich. Sergei Vasilyevich."

After injecting, it all faded away at once.

*17th January.*

There's a blizzard—no surgery. During abstinence I read a psychiatry textbook and it made a horrifying impression on me. I'm done for, there's no hope.

During abstinence, I'm frightened of rustling noises, people are hateful to me. I'm afraid of them. During the euphoria I love them all, but I prefer solitude.

Here I have to be cautious—there's a *feldsher* and two midwives here. I have to be very careful so as not to give myself away. I've become experienced, and won't do so. No one will find out while I have a supply of morphine. I prepare solutions myself or send a prescription to Anna well in advance. Once she made an attempt (an absurd one) to substitute a two-per cent solution for a five-per cent one. She brought it from Levkovo herself in freezing cold and a snowstorm.

And we had a serious quarrel because of it during the night. I convinced her not to do it. I've informed the staff here that I'm ill. I racked my brains for a long time over what illness to invent. I said I had rheumatic legs and severe neurasthenia. They've been notified that I'm going on leave to Moscow in February for treatment. Things are going smoothly. There have been no failures at work. I avoid operating on the days when I start having uncontrolled vomiting and hiccups. And so I had to give myself intestinal catarrh as well. Ah, that's too many illnesses in a single man!

The staff here are compassionate and are themselves urging me to go on leave.

External appearance: thin, and pale with a waxen pallor.

I took a bath and at the same time weighed myself on the hospital scales. Last year I weighed four poods, and now three poods, fifteen pounds.* I took fright when I looked at the arrow, but it passed.

There are incessant boils on my forearms, and the same on my thighs. I don't know how to prepare sterile solu-

*A pood was equivalent to forty Russian pounds (approximately 16 kilograms).
—Trans.

tions, and apart from that I injected myself two or three times with a syringe that hadn't been boiled, I was in a great hurry before the journey.

That's inadmissible.

*18th January.*

I had the following hallucination:

I'm expecting pale people of some sort to appear at the black windows. It's unbearable. There's only one blind. I got some gauze from the hospital and hung it as a curtain. I couldn't think up a pretext.

Oh, damn it! Why, when all's said and done, do I have to think up a pretext for my every action? I mean, it really is torment, not a life!

Am I expressing my thoughts smoothly? I think I am.

A life? Ridiculous!

*19th January.*

In an interval during surgery today, while we were relaxing and smoking in the pharmacy, the *feldsher*, twisting the powders around, told (for some reason laughing) of how a female *feldsher* suffering from morphine addiction, who had no opportunity to get hold of any morphine, used to take half a glass of laudanum. I didn't know where to look during this agonizing story. What's funny in that? It's hateful to me. What's funny about it? What?

49

I left the pharmacy with the gait of a thief.

"What do you find funny about this affliction? …"

But I restrained myself, restra—

In my situation it doesn't do to be particularly haughty with people.

Ah, the *feldsher*. He's just as cruel as those psychiatrists, who don't know how to help a sick man at all.

Not at all.

Not at all.

The preceding lines were written during abstinence, and there's a lot in them that's unfair,

It's a moonlit night now. I'm lying down, weak after an attack of vomiting. I can't lift my arms up high and I'm jotting my thoughts down in pencil. They're pure and proud. For a few hours I'm happy. Ahead of me is sleep. Above me is the moon, and on it there's a crown. Nothing's to be feared after an injection.

*1st February.*

Anna's come. She's yellow, sick.

I've finished her off. Finished her off. Yes, there's a great sin on my conscience.

I swore to her that I was leaving in the middle of February.

Will I keep my word?

Yes. I will.

If I'm alive.

*3rd February.*

And so. A hill. Icy and endless, like the one from which the fairy-tale character Kay was taken by the sledge as a child.* My last flight down that hill, and I know what awaits me at the bottom.

Oh, Anna, there'll soon be great sorrow for you, if you loved me …

*11th February.*

This is what I've decided. I'll appeal to Bomgard. Why him specifically? Because he's not a psychiatrist, because he's young and a university comrade. He's healthy and strong, but gentle, if I'm right. I remember him. Maybe he'll be … I'll find sympathy in him. He'll think of something. Let him take me to Moscow. I can't go to him. I've already had leave. I'm in bed. I don't go to the hospital.

I slandered the *feldsher*. He laughed, so what … It's not important. He came to see me. Offered to listen to me.

I didn't let him. More pretexts for the refusal? I don't want to think up a pretext.

The note to Bomgard has been sent.

People! Will someone help me?

*In Hans Christian Andersen's *The Snow Queen*. —Trans.

I've started emotional exclamations. And if anyone were to read this, they'd think it insincere. But no one will.

Before writing to Bomgard, I ran through everything in my mind. What came up in particular was the station in Moscow in November when I was fleeing from Moscow. What a dreadful evening. I was injecting stolen morphine in a lavatory … It's torment. They were trying to force their way in, there's the thundering of voices like iron, they're cursing me for keeping the place engaged for a long time, and my hands are jerking, and the catch is jerking, the next thing you know, the door'll fly open …

It's since then I've had furuncles.

I cried in the night at the memory of it.

*12th, during the night.*

And cr. again. Why this weakness and loathsomeness during the night?

*1918. 13th February at dawn in Gorelovka.*

I can congratulate myself; I've already gone fourteen hours without an injection! It's an unthinkable figure. Day is breaking, turbid and whitish. Will I be perfectly well now?

On second thoughts: I don't need Bomgard, nor anyone else. It would be shameful to extend my life even for a minute. A life like this—no, I mustn't. I have medicine to hand. Why didn't I think of it before?

Well, let's make a start. I don't owe anyone anything.

I've destroyed only myself. And Anna. What can I do?

Time will heal, as Amner. used to sing. Where she's concerned, of course, it's straightforward and simple.

The notebook goes to Bomgard. That's it ...

# V

At dawn on 14th February 1918 in a distant little town I read these, Sergei Polyakov's diary entries. And here they are in full, without any alterations whatsoever. I'm not a psychiatrist, I can't say with certainty whether they're instructive, whether they're needed. I think they are needed.

Now, when ten years have passed, the pity and fear elicited by the entries have, of course, gone. That's natural, but, having reread these notes now, when Polyakov's body has long rotted away, and all memory of him has disappeared, I have kept an interest in him. Maybe they are needed? I make so bold as to come to an affirmative decision. Anna K. died of typhus in 1922 in that same rural district where she worked. Amneris—Polyakov's first wife—is abroad.

And won't return.

Can I publish these notes, given to me as a gift?

I can. I'm publishing them. Dr Bomgard.

Autumn 1927